Published by Top That! Publishing plc
Tide Mill Way, Woodbridge, Suffolk, IP12 1AP, UK
www.topthatpublishing.com
Copyright © 2012 Top That! Publishing plc
All rights reserved
0 2 4 6 8 9 7 5 3 1
Printed and bound in China

Creative Director – Simon Couchman
Editorial Director – Daniel Graham

Written by Oakley Graham
Book illustrations by Alexia Orkrania
Cover, page 1 and 61 illustrations by Mr Henry Fisher

ISBN 978-1-84956-723-7

A catalogue record for this book is available from the British Library
Printed and bound in China

When I dream of

Polar Bear.

Polar bears are big and white and
can sometimes be a bit grumpy.
If you meet a grumpy polar bear,
build a funny snowman to cheer him up.

Wizards.

Wizards are jolly fellows with long grey beards and pointy hats. Wizards cannot hear very well on account of all the hair growing out of their ears.

Hippos.

Hippos have very sensitive skin
and love wallowing in oozy mud.
If you ever see a sunburnt hippo,
try not to laugh as this can make
them turn even redder.

Dinosaurs.

Dinosaurs are very good at hiding and so everyone thinks they are extinct. If you find a dinosaur hiding under your bed, it is best to sleep somewhere else.

Princesses.

Princesses are very pretty
and like to wear long dresses
when they go out to the shops.
Some princesses kiss frogs to see if
they will turn into a handsome prince.

Whales.

Whales are very, very big, and have very deep voices. Always stand back when a whale burps as their breath can smell rather fishy.

Pirates.

All pirates have pet parrots and mostly wear pyjamas. Pirates love to fight and never say sorry.

Penguins.

Penguins like two things;
sliding and swimming. Because
they have large feet, they are
very good at both.

Teddy Bears.

Teddy bears are kind and cuddlesome. They meet up with their friends when you are asleep and like to eat custard sandwiches.

Ladybirds.

Most ladybirds are bright red with black spots. Despite their name, not all ladybirds are ladies and no ladybirds are birds.

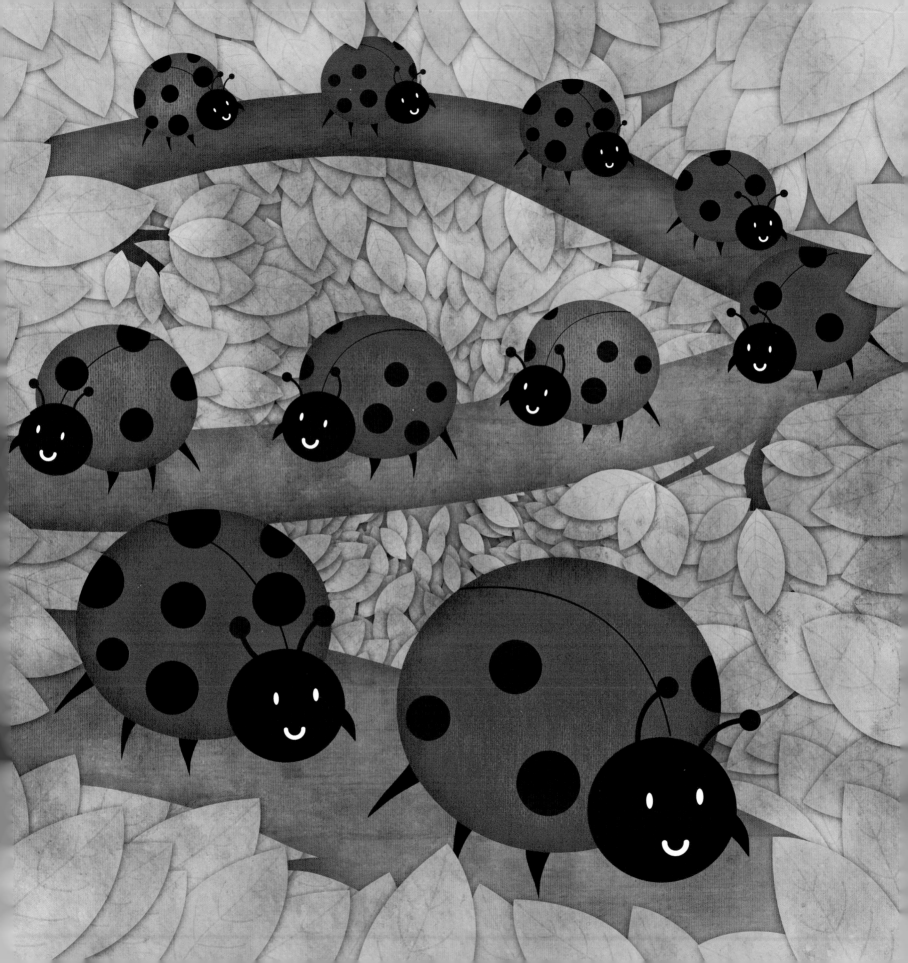

Meerkats.

Meerkats like eating crunchy bugs
and wrestling. Because of this,
their burrows tend to be rather messy.

12

Hot-Air Balloons.

Flying in a hot-air balloon is a brilliant day out. Remember to always go to the toilet before you take off, as it can take a long time to get down.

Dolphins.

Dolphins live in the sea and eat
fish. Dolphins love to tell jokes and they
brush their teeth three times a day.

Clouds.

Clouds come in lots of different shapes, colours and sizes. Although they sometimes look fluffy and pink, they do not taste like candyfloss.

Sea Horses.

Sea horses like two things;
swimming forwards and swimming
backwards. Because they are rather
small, they never get very far.

Pixies.

Pixies are the same size as a
daisy and have lots of freckles.
If you are quick enough to count a pixie's
freckles, they will grant you a wish.

Diamonds.

Diamonds always sparkle and twinkle in the light. Most queens have lots of diamonds and get very cross if the king does not buy them more for their birthday.

Jellies.

Jellies are made from special
wobbly ingredients. Despite being
so wobbly, jellies don't fall over
very often and taste great
with ice cream.

Books.

All books have a beginning, a middle and an end. It is best to start reading a book at the beginning, followed by the middle, and then finish at the end.

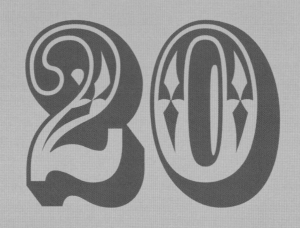

Rabbits.

Rabbits have big, floppy ears and like to work with magicians. Make sure that you have a good supply of carrots if you invite a rabbit round for tea.

Sheep.

Sheep look like fluffy clouds with legs. On account of sheep being rather boring, if you have trouble sleeping it is recommended that you try counting them.

40

Goblins.

Goblins are small and green and very naughty. Most goblins eat with their fingers and never say please or thank you.

Clownfish.

Clownfish do not dress in funny
clothes or do silly things to make
you laugh. Despite their name,
they are nothing like real clowns at all.

Ants.

Ants are very small and have lots
of brothers and sisters.
They are always busy and never
have time to go to parties.

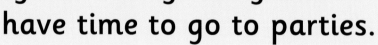

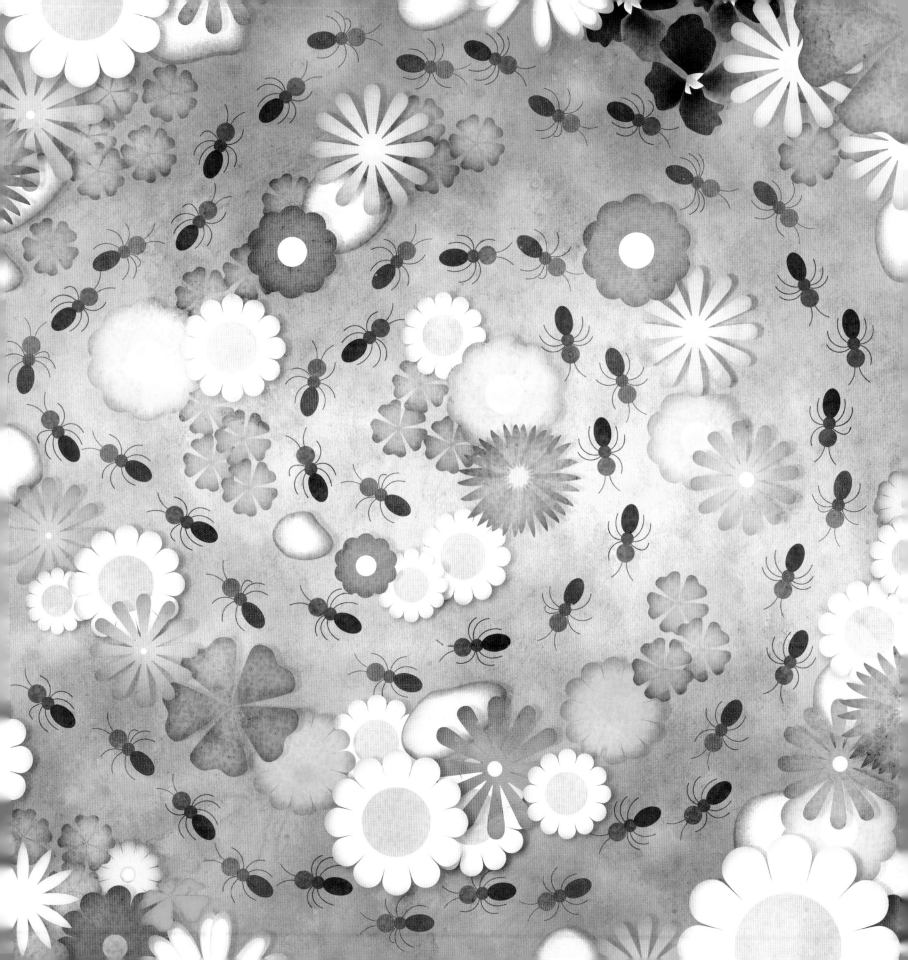

Snowflakes.

Snowflakes are cold and wet and
can mostly be seen in winter.
Snowflakes are a great invention
and can be used to make
fun things like snowmen
and snowballs.

80

Raindrops.

Raindrops travel across the sky in clouds. When a cloud gets tired, the raindrops have to get off and fall to the ground.

90

Flowers.

A flower's main job is to look pretty and to feed the bees. Some flowers are quite mischievous and like to make people sneeze.

100

Stars.

When I dream of 123, I see twinkling stars. If you ever see a shooting star, close your eyes and make a wish.

Sleep tight and goodnight ...

If you enjoyed this book, then you'll love *When I Dream of ABC*.

ISBN 978-1-84956-489-2

Children will love to learn their alphabet with this magical storybook.

Winner of *The People's Book Prize Children's Award*

'Of all the alphabet books I have seen,
When I Dream of ABC has my vote as the most
fun to read with small children.'
The Telegraph Magazine